Dear Parents:

Congratulations! Your child is taking the first steps on an exciting journey. The destination? Independent reading!

STEP INTO READING® will help your child get there. The program offers five steps to reading success. Each step includes fun stories and colorful art or photographs. In addition to original fiction and books with favorite characters, there are Step into Reading Non-Fiction Readers, Phonics Readers and Boxed Sets, Sticker Readers, and Comic Readers—a complete literacy program with something to interest every child.

Learning to Read, Step by Step!

Ready to Read   Preschool–Kindergarten
• big type and easy words • rhyme and rhythm • picture clues
For children who know the alphabet and are eager to begin reading.

Reading with Help   Preschool–Grade 1
• basic vocabulary • short sentences • simple stories
For children who recognize familiar words and sound out new words with help.

Reading on Your Own   Grades 1–3
• engaging characters • easy-to-follow plots • popular topics
For children who are ready to read on their own.

Reading Paragraphs   Grades 2–3
• challenging vocabulary • short paragraphs • exciting stories
For newly independent readers who read simple sentences with confidence.

Ready for Chapters   Grades 2–4
• chapters • longer paragraphs • full-color art
For children who want to take the plunge into chapter books but still like colorful pictures.

STEP INTO READING® is designed to give every child a successful reading experience. The grade levels are only guides; children will progress through the steps at their own speed, developing confidence in their reading.

Remember, a lifetime love of reading starts with a single step!

Special thanks to Ryan Ferguson, Debra Mostow Zakarin, Sammie Suchland, Kristine Lombardi, Nicole Corse, Karen Painter, Stuart Smith, Charnita Belcher, Julia Phelps, Julia Pistor, Renata Marchand, Garrett Sander, Kris Fogel, Rachael Datello, Michael Goguen, Lauren Rose, Sarah Serata, and Rainmaker Entertainment

Published in the United States by Random House Children's Books, a division of Penguin Random House LLC, 1745 Broadway, New York, NY 10019, and in Canada by Penguin Random House Canada Limited, Toronto.

Visit us on the Web!
StepIntoReading.com
randomhousekids.com

Educators and librarians, for a variety of teaching tools, visit us at RHTeachersLibrarians.com

ISBN 978-0-399-55858-0 (trade) — ISBN 978-0-399-55859-7 (lib. bdg.)

Printed in the United States of America
10 9 8 7 6 5 4 3 2 1

Random House Children's Books supports the First Amendment and celebrates the right to read.

Barbie
VIDEO GAME HERO

RACE FOR THE STARS

Adapted by Jennifer Liberts

Based on the screenplay by Nina Bargiel
with additional writing by Jennifer Skelly

Illustrated by Elisabetta Melaranci,
Patrizia Zangrilli, and Ann Beliashova

Random House 🏠 New York

Barbie likes

to play video games.

She plays

with her friends.

One day,
Barbie is pulled
into the game!

The game has a virus.
Cutie asks Barbie
to beat the virus.
She will help!

Barbie starts

to play.

She meets other players.

They want
to beat Barbie!

She helps the others.
Barbie must win every
level to beat the virus.

The others help Barbie.

Barbie wins Level One!

In Level Two,
Barbie turns
into a sticker.

Barbie saves
a girl in a tree.
She beats Level Two!

13

Barbie is worried.

The virus

is getting stronger.

In the final level,
Barbie changes
into pixels.

Cutie asks Barbie
to change the game
with her special codes.

The virus bursts
into the final level.

The team makes
an anti-virus.
Barbie blasts the virus
with it.

Barbie stops the virus.

She wins the final level!

But the virus turns

into a super virus!

Barbie changes the game.
She uses her <u>own</u> code
to make it a dance game!

The virus turns
into happy faces.
Barbie beats the virus!

Barbie wins
a star prize.

She saved the game
<u>and</u> made it fun!

Barbie and her sister
love playing the fun new
dance game together!